Echoes Of Us

By: Britt Wolfe

This Novella Is Dedicated to:

The couples who hold hands through history.

To every breathtaking, heartbreaking, goosebump-inducing love story I've ever witnessed—real or imagined. To the couples who make us believe in forever, even when the odds are stacked against them. To the ones who fight for love through war, time, silence, and storm. To the ones who find each other again and again, across lifetimes, in dreams and déjà vu.

And to my own other half—Sean.

You are the spark, the softness, the gravity that grounds me and the magic that lifts me higher. We may not have lived a thousand lives, but in this one?

We love like we've known each other for all of them.

Thank you to all the couples who inspire beauty, romance, and just the right touch of tragedy. You are the reason stories like this one exist. You are the reason I believe.

The Echoes Of Us
Is Inspired by: Timeless *(Taylor's Version)*
by Taylor Swift

From the first time I heard *Timeless,* I felt it settle into my chest like something ancient and aching and beautiful. To me, it's a song about a love so enduring, so destined, that even time itself bows to it. A love that survives war, outlives empires, and defies every ending it's given. A love that remembers.

As I listened, I found myself imagining a couple who just kept finding each other—across centuries, across cities, across lives. Always falling. Always loving. Always losing.

This novella is my love letter to that kind of romance—the kind that feels stitched into the stars. It's for the dreamers who believe in fate, for the hearts who ache for second chances, and for anyone who has ever felt like they were born loving someone they hadn't met yet.

And of course, it's for Sean—my once-in-a-lifetime in the only life we'll ever need. Ours is the kind of love I used to write stories about. Now, I get to live it.

I hope this story finds the ones who still believe.

Peace, Love, and Inspiration,

Britt Wolfe

The Moment Before Memory
Philadelphia, Pennsylvania ~ 2022

The station was all light and shadow and sound.

Sunlight filtered through the tall arched windows in long, golden beams, dust spinning slowly within them like snow in a shaken snow globe. The stone columns stood sentinel along the perimeter of the grand hall, each one reaching toward a ceiling so high it seemed to carry the echoes of the past. Soft murmurs floated up and dissolved there—footsteps and laughter, the roll of suitcase wheels, the low call of a departing train.

Outside, the city pulsed with March chill and muted grey, but inside 30th Street Station, it was warm and humming, wrapped in the quiet reverence of movement and pause.

She stood near the far window, bundled in a camel-coloured coat, hands curled around a paper cup of black coffee that had long since gone cold. Around her, the world pressed forward—travellers rushing home, lovers reuniting with breathless embraces, children twirling in the open space as pigeons flapped lazily above the marble.

But she didn't move. Not yet.

There was something in the stillness here. Something old. Something watchful.

She'd always loved places like this—places that held beginnings and endings in equal measure. There was something sacred about the threshold of a train station, the way people arrived and departed, always on the verge of somewhere, of something. It made her feel less alone. Like even if you weren't going anywhere, you still could.

Her gaze wandered slowly, painting the scene in her mind like she always did: the glow of the chandeliers overhead, their light catching in brass railings and polished floors; the ripple of a red scarf in the distance; the shifting dance of strangers weaving in and out of each other's lives.

And then, she saw him.

He was standing beneath the departures board, unmoving. One hand in the pocket of his coat, the other curled loosely around the strap of a worn leather satchel. He wasn't remarkable at first glance—tall, with the wind still in his hair and something about him that felt a little misplaced, like he hadn't yet landed in this century. But it wasn't his presence that caught her.

It was the feeling.

The kind that grips you in the ribs before your mind can name it. The way your body knows before your heart dares to hope.

She blinked. Watched him shift his weight. Tilt his head as though listening for something in the air.

And then he looked at her.

Their eyes met across the distance.

And the world... *tipped*.

Just slightly. Like a painting gone crooked. Like time itself had inhaled and forgotten how to exhale.

She forgot the coffee cup in her hand. Forgot the chill in the air or the chatter around her. All she could feel was that gaze—steady, familiar, impossible. Her throat tightened. Her chest ached like an old bruise pressed too hard.

She didn't know him.

But she knew him.

Her skin flushed cold and warm at once, a static hum beginning at the base of her spine and crawling upward.

He blinked, once. Took a step forward.

She mirrored him without thinking.

And then—

A crowd passed between them. The moment shattered like glass. Voices rose. Someone laughed. A suitcase rolled too loud across the floor.

When the space cleared, he was gone.

Her heart was racing. Her body trembling. Her breath caught on something she couldn't explain.

She turned in slow circles, scanning the crowd, but there was no trace of him. No name to call. No reason to chase.

Only the whisper in her bones that she had just missed something she'd been waiting lifetimes to find.

She closed her eyes.

And the silence said: not yet. But soon.

The First Time They Loved
Tudor England ~ 1538

It was early enough that the mist still kissed the hedgerows.

Soft grey light filtered through the latticework of the east-facing corridor, where the castle walls gave way to ivy-covered stone and the outline of a hidden garden. The rest of the palace hadn't yet stirred—not the kitchens with their fire-scorched hearths, not the chapel bells, not the chambermaids who whispered secrets as they folded linens and swept away yesterday's ash.

But the woman was awake. She moved like a breath through the hallway, slippers silent on the worn flagstones, one hand gathering the hem of her gown to keep it from dragging through the morning damp.

The door that led to the Queen's private garden had long since fallen out of use, but she had found it anyway. She always did. It was tucked behind a crooked tapestry, one frayed corner stitched with a forgotten crest, and behind it—an old latch, stiff with time. She had pulled it once, months ago, when everything in her life felt too loud, too watched, too decided. And what had opened before her had been nothing short of holy.

A garden, yes. But not a court garden. Not clipped and pruned and perfected for the eyes of nobles.

This was a secret. A hush. A living, breathing wildness, grown in defiance of order.

The woman stepped into it now, and the breath left her lungs.

There was a softness to the world here. The kind that only came in the breath between night and day, when the dew had not yet surrendered to sun, when petals remained curled as if still dreaming. A low fog floated just above the ground, wrapping itself around the tangled roses and foxglove, curling beneath the stone bench near the pear tree. The air smelled of green things and something older—lavender, sage, the ghost of something herbal and healing.

She came here to think. Or more truthfully, to not think.

To feel instead.

And this morning, as she crossed beneath the arch of ivy and ran her fingers across the rough stone, she felt something shift in her chest. Something new.

He was there.

A man, half in shadow, seated on the edge of the old stone bench with a book resting in his lap and a half-crushed sprig of thyme tucked between its pages.

She froze, heart climbing into her throat.

He didn't move. Didn't notice her, not yet. The candle tucked into the lantern beside him was unlit, and he was reading only by the light of dawn, his head tilted forward, hair tumbling loose at his brow. His tunic was plain but clean, sleeves rolled to his elbows. His fingers—long, steady—rested lightly against the page.

He looked... peaceful.

And she, uninvited, was suddenly afraid to breathe.

Her first instinct was to leave. To melt back into the corridor, unseen. But then—

He looked up.

And everything in her changed.

It wasn't that he was beautiful, though he was. It was the way he looked at her. Not like she was the lady-in-waiting to the Queen of England. Not like she was the daughter of a fallen noble house, poised for a strategic marriage to restore what her father had squandered. Not like she was a name or a reputation or a crown waiting to be claimed.

He looked at her like she was real.

Their eyes held. A single, breathless second. Maybe two.

Then he stood.

Slowly. No rush. No panic. Just the graceful unfolding of a man entirely at ease with stillness.

"I didn't think this place was known to many, Queen Lady." he said.

His voice was low. Gentle. With the soft edges of someone from the North —Yorkshire, maybe, but softened by education. Polished.

She stepped closer. "It isn't. How did you find it?"

He smiled—small, slow. Like the sunrise coming through fog.

"I followed the quiet."

She wanted to smile back. But her lips couldn't quite move. Her body was too full of the moment—of the scent of thyme, and old paper, and the way he was looking at her now, like he already knew something she hadn't yet dared to name.

His book slipped closed between his hands. "May I ask your name?"

"You already know it."

"Do I?"

"You called me the Queen's lady. You must have seen me before."

"I have," he admitted. "But knowing a name is not the same as knowing a person."

She tilted her head, emboldened. "And your name?"

"The man," he said, simply.

Just that. No title. No House.

Nothing to anchor him in the world she came from.

But somehow... he felt more real than anyone she'd ever met in it.

She came closer.

The fog stirred around her ankles. The sun caught in the loose strands of her hair.

And somewhere, in the deepest part of her chest, something clicked softly into place.

*****

They met again the next day.

Not by arrangement, but by something more binding. A thread pulling through time, invisible and undeniable.

The woman didn't ask why he was there. The man didn't ask why she'd returned. They simply found one another among the green, beneath the bloom-heavy boughs and the hush of leaves turning toward sun.

He brought his book again. She brought the sound of her laughter, rare and light, unguarded.

They spoke in pieces. Stories shared in sips, like fine wine.

He told her of music, of songsmiths and luthiers and the way a note could live longer than a body. She told him of books, of her mother's gentle voice reciting Chaucer before sleep, of stolen parchment and ink-stained fingertips.

And slowly, their words became warmth.

They shared the garden for weeks. Always in the early hush. Always in secret.

And in those golden-lit mornings, with petals brushing her skirts and the scent of rosemary clinging to his sleeves, they began to fall in love.

Not loudly. Not quickly.

But in the way vines climb stone. Sure. Steady.

Certain.

And in every glance, in every breathless pause between words, the promise of more hung in the air like jasmine.

They just didn't know what more would cost them.

Not yet.

Not then.

*****

It was late when they saw each other again.

Not in the garden, but within the quiet hush of the chapel corridor, where candlelight flickered like breath and shadows clung to the corners like secrets. The woman had slipped away after supper, the weight of expectation pressing too tightly against her ribs. She wandered without destination, but her feet seemed to know where to carry her.

And there he was.

The man.

A single taper lit the alcove where he stood, hands dusted with chalk from the fresco he was sketching. He had not heard her approach, but when he turned, it was as though he'd known she was coming all along.

Neither spoke.

She moved first—slowly, deliberately—closing the distance until the space between them was made only of breath. He set the charcoal down. The tension of restraint flickered in his jaw.

Then her fingers reached for his.

And he broke.

The kiss was reverent.

Soft at first. A brushing of mouths like pages turning. But the moment it deepened, the world fell away. He pulled her to him with hands that had learned her in silence, fingers tracing the line of her back, writing her into memory.

She pressed him against the stone wall, her lips parting beneath his, her hands tangling in the fabric at his collar. The chamber was cold, but her skin burned where he touched it, his palms moving beneath the layers of her gown to find the curve of her waist, the heat of her skin.

They broke apart only to breathe, foreheads pressed together.

"Tell me to stop," he whispered.

She answered him with a kiss.

The chamber behind the corridor was barely large enough to contain them, but it had walls, and a door, and a bolt that slid into place with a click that sounded like fate. The woman lit the candle on the table with trembling hands, and the man turned her gently toward the wall, undoing the tiny pearl buttons at the nape of her gown with slow, measured reverence.

Fabric fell to the floor, whispering like a secret.

His hands followed, drawing hallowed lines down the bare length of her back. She turned to him, unashamed, eyes wide with trust and something deeper—something crimson and primally human.

He kissed her slowly, devoutly, like a man discovering the divine.

Her fingers found the edge of his tunic, pulling it over his head, revealing skin that flushed under the glow of candlelight. When he lifted her, her legs wrapped around his hips like they had done so a thousand times before.

He laid her down among their discarded cloaks and pressed his body to hers with aching patience. When he entered her, it was not with urgency, but wonder.

She gasped.

He stilled.

Their eyes locked, and she nodded—just once.

He moved inside her like music. Like prayer.

Their breaths tangled. Their hands searched. Their mouths found each other again and again, as if the world might end before they had enough of one another.

And when they shattered together—his name unspoken, hers caught in the catch of his breath—it felt like something greater had risen up to witness them.

They lay together after, curled in the hush of their sacred space, her cheek pressed to his chest, his fingers brushing idle paths across her shoulder.

"If this is all we're allowed," she whispered, "let it be enough."

He kissed her brow.

"In another life," he murmured, "we are never torn apart."

But even then, the candle flickered.

Even then, the silence began to change.

Even then, the world was listening.

*****

It was the Queen's advisor who found them.

A whisper in the wrong ear. A misstep in a quiet hall.

The man was seized before the sun rose, dragged from the chapel with bloodied lip and bound hands.

The woman was confined to her chamber. No explanations. No chance to scream. No final goodbye.

And when she pressed her ear to the door and heard the bells ring midday, she knew what it meant.

She tried to claw her way out.

She screamed until her throat bled.

But by the time she reached the courtyard—barefoot, breathless, undone —

He was gone.

No trial. No mercy. Only the blade, and the silence that followed it.

The woman fell to her knees in the place where his blood had soaked the earth. Her sob was not a sound, but a fracture. A breaking. A soul being torn from what it had waited lifetimes to find.

It was raining.

No one spoke to her. No one dared.

And when she rose, something in her eyes had changed.

Something ancient. Something hollow. Something broken apart.

They married her off before the season's end.

A duke. Older. Cold.

She smiled at the ceremony.

She carried the man's child to term in silence, though the duke never knew.

And every year, on the day the bells rang, she returned to the garden.

Alone.

She whispered nothing.

She laid her palm to the stone bench.

And still, even through the ivy and the hush of passing time—
It remembered him.

She did too.

Because love like theirs never disappears.

It waits.

It carries on.

Until it finds its way again.

In another life.

In another story.

In another chance to begin.

The market was alive with colour and rain.

Thin threads of mist wove through the canopies like breath, softening the edges of things, making the whole world feel slightly out of focus. Fabric tents flapped gently overhead in a quilted patchwork of stripes and florals, their corners weighted with twine and rusted bells that chimed whenever the wind stirred. Beneath them, the stalls bloomed with riotous abundance—ruby-skinned apples, bouquets of chamomile and sweet pea, jars of raw honey, loaves of bread still warm from the oven.

The air smelled of rosemary and wet pavement and yeast. Somewhere nearby, a jazz trio played beneath a faded blue awning, their notes dancing through the drizzle, threading through the hum of conversation, the rustle of brown paper bags, the hiss of tires on damp asphalt.

He didn't know why he had come.

He'd meant to walk off the heaviness that had been clinging to him all morning, the way it sometimes did—like memory, but not. Like déjà vu, but deeper. The kind of weight you carry in your bones when you've been waiting for something without knowing what.

So he walked.

Hands buried in the pockets of his coat, collar turned up against the mist, breath rising in pale curls. He passed a row of heirloom tomatoes, a stall of hand-carved wooden spoons. He paused at a crate of peaches, lifted one absently to his nose. Sweetness. Summer. Something familiar.

And then he saw her.

She was standing at a flower stall halfway down the row, bent slightly at the waist, her hand hovering over a table of peonies. Not yet touching. Just... hovering. As though trying to memorize the moment before touch. Her umbrella hung loosely from her wrist, forgotten. Water droplets clung to the curve of her hair, the bridge of her nose, the collar of her linen dress.

She looked... serene.

Unaware of everything else. As if the rest of the world had fallen away. As if only the flowers existed. And she, among them.

He stopped walking.

His chest clenched—not with panic, but with the sharp, silent recognition that steals your breath before your mind can catch it.

He knew her.

Not her name. Not the shape of her lips as she spoke. But there was a deep and ancient familiarity. Something carved into him.

He stood very still.

She reached forward and lifted a bloom from the bunch. Pale pink, thick-petaled, almost luminous in the grey light. She brought it to her nose. Closed her eyes. Smiled—not for anyone else. Just for the flower. For herself.

And just like that—

A door opened inside him.

He remembered a garden.

He remembered a girl.

He remembered her.

Ink-stained fingers. Candlelight flickering across stone. Laughter in the ivy. The rustle of skirts. The scrape of parchment.

He remembered the feel of her in his arms.

The scent of lavender and smoke.

A cry. A blade. A scream.

His knees nearly buckled.

She looked up then.

Straightening slowly, as if sensing the shift in the air. Her gaze swept the crowd, unhurried, until it landed on him.

Their eyes met.

And the world....*slipped*.

Folded in on itself. Just a little.

The market kept moving—umbrellas bobbing, bags rustling, music playing—but none of it touched them.

Her expression shifted. Something rippled through her face—recognition, disbelief, fear. All tangled together. She blinked. Her fingers loosened. The peony slipped from her grasp.

He took a step forward.

Only one.

But it was enough to tip something in the air.

A woman with a stroller wheeled between them.

A man with a basket of oranges bumped his shoulder, offered a quick apology.

And when he looked again—

She was gone.

Just... gone.

The space where she had stood felt hollow.

The vendor behind the table looked up at him with a mild, curious frown. "You okay?"

He blinked. Tried to speak.

"Did you see where she went?"

The vendor glanced left, then right. "Which one?"

He couldn't answer. His throat was dry. His heart was thudding. He stepped forward slowly, stopping at the place where she had stood just moments ago. The fabric of the canopy swayed overhead. The scent of the peonies was stronger here—green and sweet and vaguely sad.

There, at his feet, lay the flower she had dropped.

He crouched.

Picked it up.

Turned it gently in his fingers like it might give him an answer.

The petals were bruised where it had landed. Softened at the edges. He held it as though it were precious, as though it had always belonged to him.

And then—without knowing why—he closed his eyes.

His mind whispered a name he didn't remember learning.

The rain came harder.

He stood there for a long time, the flower cupped in his hand.

And the wind moved through the market like a hush.

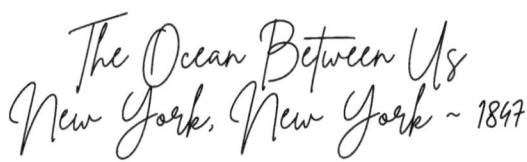
The ship groaned as it docked, wood strained and ropes snapping taut as though the vessel itself were reluctant to release its cargo. Fog clung to the harbour like breath, wrapping the city in a veil of wet grey. From the deck, everything looked carved in charcoal—the rooftops, the chimneys, the buildings crowded along the water's edge.

She stepped onto American soil with a lace-edged handkerchief clutched tightly in her palm, a younger cousin pressed close at her side, and a hunger in her belly that had become so familiar she no longer noticed it. Her shoes were worn so thin they barely held together. Every step landed straight into the stone.

They didn't speak. There was nothing to say. The city around them was loud—languages she couldn't understand, voices sharp with urgency, wagons rattling, dockworkers shouting, men barking orders from the shore. The air smelled of ash and meat and salt and something sour beneath it all, like a wound that wouldn't heal.

She kept her head down.

*****

Later, outside a chapel that smelled of candle wax and boiled cabbage, she bent over a crate of second-hand clothes, searching for something dry to wear. Her cousin waited nearby with a blanket over her shoulders, eyes wide and quiet.

She didn't notice him at first.

Not until she felt it—that uncanny stillness.

She looked up.

And there he was.

He stood near the soup line, coat patched at the elbows, jaw shadowed with stubble, a bundle of firewood slung over one shoulder. He was younger than most of the labourers, but older in the eyes. He looked at her like she was something he remembered from a dream he hadn't known he'd forgotten.

For a moment, the world stopped moving.

The city was loud.

But in that second, all she heard was his breath.

Someone shoved past her. A man dropped a ladle. Her cousin coughed.

She blinked. He was still there.

Their eyes didn't break.

He didn't smile. Neither did she. But something passed between them.

Like a thread pulled taut.

And then he turned.

And walked away.

*****

She saw him again the following week. Her fingers were raw from scrubbing the bakery floors, her wrists sore from lifting crates of flour. The streets were always damp. Her apron was never clean.

He was loading barrels onto a wagon. One slipped, and he caught it with a grunt and a curse.

She knelt beside him before she knew she'd moved.

"Your hand," she said softly.

He didn't flinch.

Just offered it, bloodied knuckles and all.

She tore a strip from the hem of her skirt and wrapped it around his palm. Carefully. Slowly.

"Thank you," he murmured.

She didn't answer.

Their hands touched longer than they needed to.

That night, he waited outside the bakery. She stepped into the alley at the end of her shift, breath clouding in the cold, fingers trembling at the sight of him.

They walked.

Through streets strung with laundry and lanterns, past doors that opened onto stairwells of music and grief. They didn't say much. Didn't need to. The silence stretched between them like an invitation.

He pointed out constellations.

She told him about the name of the ship that had brought her over.

"The Morning Star," she said.

He nodded. "Of course it was."

*****

Weeks passed.

She began to laugh again, a strange sound from her mouth into the gritty air of this strange country. Her joy was soft, at first. And, only when he was near.

He started leaving things for her. A sprig of thyme. A coin engraved with a clover. A torn page from a prayer book tucked into the bakery doorframe.

She stitched the tear in his only shirt.

He left her a scarf, mended with green thread.

They made a home in alleyways and half-whispered confessions.

And then, one night, he followed her up the stairs to a room above the bakery.

The hall creaked beneath their feet. The scent of warm yeast and ash clung to the floorboards, and the only light came from the lantern she carried in her hand. The flame flickered with each breath, casting gold across the peeling walls, the curve of her shoulder, the sharp line of his jaw.

The room was barely wide enough for a bed and basin. The window rattled. The plaster cracked near the corners. But in that moment, it felt like a cathedral.

She set the lantern on the sill and turned slowly. Her fingers trembled. Not from fear—but from something deeper. Something that lived beneath the skin, beneath the ribcage, something ancient as breath.

He didn't speak.

He stepped inside like he was afraid to wake her.

And when she reached for the ribbon at her throat, he caught her hand.

Not to stop her.

Just to feel it happen.

Their clothes fell in pieces. Slowly. With reverence. Her shawl slipped to the floor like a whisper. His shirt peeled away with the sound of fabric worn too thin. He was lean, sun-marked, bruised in places no one ever touched.

She pressed her lips to one of them.

He exhaled, sharp and ragged.

She traced a scar along his shoulder, and he let her. Quietly. Eyes closed. Her fingers were soft. Searching.

He kissed the back of her hand—once. Then again.

And when he bent to kiss her neck, it was with something that felt like prayer.

Their mouths met—not with hunger, but with ache.

When he cupped her face, she leaned into it. When she tugged him closer, his breath caught. And when she slipped her dress from her shoulders, he watched it fall like he'd never seen anything more holy.

The bed creaked beneath them.

The sheets were thin, but their bodies made warmth.

He touched her like he already knew her. Like he remembered the map of her collarbones. The curve of her hip. The small hollow behind her knee.

She gasped when his mouth found her breast.

He murmured her name like it was the only word he'd ever known.

When he entered her, it was slow. Devastating. Her legs wrapped around his waist, her hands in his hair, and the air between them thick with everything they hadn't said.

Their rhythm built in soft waves—gentle at first. Hesitant. Then deeper. Surer. Like a story being rewritten in skin.

She arched into him, and he broke apart for her.

Her moan was a memory made flesh.

His name on her lips undid him.

Their bodies learned each other the way hunger learns quiet. The way exiles find prayer.

And when they finally reached the height of their pleasure, it was together.

Chest to chest.

Mouth to mouth.

Breath to breath.

"I've had nothing," he murmured, voice caught in her neck. "Until you."

*****

They were saving.

Pennies folded into the lining of her apron. Coins tucked behind loose bricks.

She would be free of her debt by spring.

They would leave the city. Start somewhere new. Somewhere quiet. Somewhere green.

They had a plan.

She kissed it into his mouth every night.

He carved it into her bones with his hands.

But plans are small things in a cruel world.

*****

It was the first warm evening of spring. The kind of evening that made the city breathe a little easier, when coats were left open and windows cracked to let in the smell of rain-softened earth. She had braided her red hair. Worn the scarf he had mended with the green thread. Tucked their savings into a hidden pocket in her skirt. A satchel rested at her feet. Inside, her best blouse, a loaf of bread, and a crumpled prayer card.

She waited outside the tavern, just beyond the iron gate on Orchard Street, where they'd agreed to meet.

The clover coin was tight in her palm.

He was late.

She shifted her weight. Looked up the street. Tucked a loose strand of hair behind her ear.

That's when the offender approached.

He was heavy in his steps, sweat beading at his temple despite the cool dusk. His shirt hung loose around his belly, stained and stretched. His eyes scanned her like she was something for sale in a market, his tongue lolled from his lips.

"Well now," the offender slurred, "don't you look like a sweet little thing waiting on her gentleman." He chuckled, and the sound made her throat close.

She said nothing. Turned her face away.

He stepped closer.

"Too fine to be standing out here alone, aren't you? Bet there's a mouth on you behind that prim little face."

Her fingers curled tighter around the coin. She tried to push him away.

He caught her elbow.

"You don't want to be rude, girl," he muttered, leaning in. "Pretty mouth like that's meant for softer things."

She shoved him. Hard.

The offender laughed. "Oh, you've got fire. Good."

And then—he grabbed her waist, tried to pull her toward him. His mouth came for hers.

But before it could land—

A shout cut through the air like a whip.

"Get your hands off her."

He was there. Her love. The one she'd been waiting for. Chest rising with fury. Eyes dark with rage. He stepped between them, shoving the offender back hard, planting himself like a wall in front of her.

"You alright?" he asked, voice trembling but steady.

She nodded, breathless. Gripping his arm.

The offender laughed and swung.

It was fast. A flash of fists. The sickening sound of knuckle meeting cheek. He dodged the first blow. Landed one of his own.

Then another.

Then—too close to the edge—he stumbled.

A final shove sent him backward.

He fell into the street.

There was a *crack* when his head hit the cobblestone.

Then stillness.

She screamed before she reached him.

The world blurred as she dropped to her knees beside him, the hem of her dress blooming red. His breath was shallow. Laboured. His eyes fluttered, searching. His lips moved but made no sound.

"No, no—no," she whispered, her voice cracking. "Stay with me. Please, stay."

He looked at her.

Really looked.

And then—he reached for her hand.

She guided his hand to the soft curve of her belly, pressing it there so he could feel the beginning she was quietly growing inside her—a future shaped in the echo of their love.

His fingers trembled.

His eyes went wide with something not quite surprise.

"You..." he managed. "You're..."

She nodded, sobbing now. "It's yours. You're going to be a father."

He smiled.

Not with joy.

With peace.

With *knowing.*

His thumb brushed her belly once.

Then fell away.

His breath stilled.

Her scream ripped through the alley like a warning.

She pulled him into her arms, pressed her face to his chest, to his neck, to his cooling lips. Rocked him like a child. Blood soaked into her dress, her sleeves, her skin.

She wept until she could no longer breathe.

When the priest came, she wouldn't let them take him.

Not until she had kissed his forehead.

Not until she had whispered his name.

Not until she had told him—again and again—that she would find him. That she always would, no matter how many lifetimes it would take.

And when she finally let go, she did so with the clover coin pressed into her fist.

She buried him herself.

There was no headstone. No eulogy.

Just the scarf he had mended with green thread, folded neatly over his chest.

Just a prayer book in his hands, bloodstained and soft with rain.

Just her name on his lips as he left.

And his on hers as she walked away.

Find me again.

The park was almost empty.

Late February, the sky low and silver, the wind biting at her cheeks. Snow had fallen the night before, and though most of it had melted by morning, a thin crust still clung to the grass and gathered in the hollows of the stone path. The trees were bare. The benches dusted with ice. And everything smelled like cold metal and woodsmoke from distant chimneys.

She didn't come here often. But something had pulled her from the apartment that afternoon—an ache, a restlessness, the kind of tug in the chest you don't question. She told herself it was to clear her head. To get some air. But the truth was, she couldn't sit still anymore.

Not with the dreams.

They were getting stronger.

The ship. The scarf. The man with rough, working hands running over her body. She'd woken breathless twice that week, her hand pressed to her chest like she was trying to keep something in.

So she walked.

Past the frozen fountain. Past the statue of the angel holding up a bowl of birds.

And that's when she saw him.

Across the lawn, standing at the edge of the footbridge, hands tucked into the pockets of a dark coat, collar turned up against the wind.

She recognized him.

She knew him.

Not just from the market the year before, or the train station before that. Not just from the dreams. Not just from the ache.

From something deeper.

He was looking out over the water. Still. Quiet. As if listening for something only he could hear.

And in that moment, the world narrowed.

The wind dropped.

The sky held its breath.

She stepped forward slowly.

One step.

Another.

And then he turned.

His profile. The shape of his mouth. The slope of his shoulders.

She had seen them all before. In flickers. In fragments. Across time. Across lives.

She opened her mouth.

But before she could speak, a group of teenagers jogged past, their laughter loud in the stillness.

She blinked.

He was gone.

The bridge was empty.

She hurried forward, snow crunching beneath her boots. Reached the railing. Looked down the path.

Nothing.

No sign of him.

Just the air, colder now. The sky a little darker.

She stood there for a long time, hands gripping the iron railing.

And whispered, "Please. Just one more time."

The wind stirred the trees.

And somewhere behind her, the sound of footsteps faded.

The Time They Almost Made It
Marcus Hook, Pennsylvania ~ 1944

The air smelled like woodsmoke and sea salt, even though the ocean was miles away.

She walked along the uneven boards of the town's main street, her hands tucked deep into the pockets of her wool coat, the cold biting through the seams. The wind carried the hush of something just beneath memory— like the echo of a song she couldn't quite recall the name of. Streetlamps buzzed above her in their wartime dimness, muted by blackout shades, casting only the softest halos of light.

This was a place suspended between two worlds—the old and the not-yet-broken. Houses lined with wraparound porches and weather-worn siding, stoops swept clean of leaves, American flags hanging solemnly in windows. Somewhere nearby, a radio crackled with the Andrews Sisters, the sound drifting like mist through the branches of bare November trees.

She had come here six months ago, answering a call she couldn't ignore. The war effort needed nurses, and the local hospital had been short-staffed since '42. The town was small, tucked against the Pennsylvania coast where the hills rolled into river valleys, not far from the Delaware Bay. There were trains here. And shipyards not too far. And men who returned with wounds no one could see.

She had tended to all of them. Wrapped bandages. Changed linens. Held hands slick with sweat from pain and memory. Sometimes they woke screaming. Sometimes they didn't wake at all.

And sometimes—

Sometimes they opened their eyes, and everything stopped.

Like the man in Room Fourteen.

He had arrived in the hush before dawn, when the air still tasted of frost and chimney smoke. Two medics carried him in, their boots loud on the linoleum, and a third clutched a clipboard, rattling off details she barely heard. Her eyes had gone to his face instead—the grime on his cheeks, the soft tremble of his jaw, the pulse fluttering beneath the curve of his throat.

He was young. Or maybe just younger than the others. His uniform was torn at the shoulder, a dark stain spreading slowly across the fabric, and in his right hand, clenched so tightly his knuckles had gone pale, was a single sheet of paper.

He wouldn't let it go.

Even as the fever set in. Even when they cut away his uniform and packed his shoulder with gauze. Even when he slipped into the kind of sleep that smelled like morphine and blood and the distance between one life and the next.

He held that paper like a lifeline.

The woman had leaned in once, just to look.

The ink was blurred. The writing small and rushed. But she could still make out the first line: *If I don't make it back, know that loving you was worth every moment.*

She hadn't looked further.

She'd simply sat beside him as he slept, one hand resting lightly on the edge of the bed, her touch not quite reaching his. She told herself it was only her shift. Only her duty. Only a patient like any other.

But still—

She waited.

She waited for him to open his eyes.

It was the third day when he did.

The ward was quiet then. Early evening. Rain tapped against the windows in soft, rhythmic pulses, and the scent of boiled potatoes lingered from the half-eaten dinner trays. The lights overhead buzzed faintly, casting long shadows on the waxed floors.

She was changing his IV. Focused. Gentle. Her fingers moved with a calm that came from repetition, from knowing how to soften pain without needing to speak.

And then—

He stirred.

A small shift of weight. A furrow at his brow. A breath caught just slightly too hard in his chest.

Her hands stilled.

Slowly, carefully, she looked down at him.

And his eyes were open.

The room did not shift. The air did not still. But something *in her* did.

His gaze wasn't frantic like most of them. It wasn't wild or lost. It was steady. Sure.

Like he had been waiting to find her.

His voice, when it came, was barely more than a breath.

"You found me."

The words landed in her like a match to dry paper.

She didn't speak.

Couldn't.

She only nodded, the movement small. And in that moment, she felt something impossible stretch between them—like thread pulled taut, tugging them together through time.

He blinked slowly, his eyes never leaving hers. Then, as if the effort had cost him everything, he slipped back into sleep.

But she didn't leave.

She sat beside him, her palm resting on the letter he still held.

And for the first time since she arrived in this town, the ache in her chest softened.

Just a little.

Like something lost had found its way back home.

*****

That first touch shifted something between them.

In the days that followed, they didn't speak of it. They didn't have to. The touch became glances held a breath too long, the pause of a hand lingering at a sleeve, the softening of footsteps as they approached one another. It was a gravity neither of them resisted, a pull they both understood instinctively—as though their bodies remembered what their minds had not yet caught up to.

He recovered slowly, but each day he grew stronger. He walked the corridor now, pacing the length of the ward with careful steps, sometimes resting his hand on the windowsill to watch the wind tousle the leaves outside. And always, when she passed him, he turned toward her like a flower to the sun.

She brought him books when he could sit long enough to read. She read aloud when the rain came. Once, she laughed at something he said—a real laugh, unguarded and bright—and he looked at her as though he had just been handed a second chance at life.

Their first kiss was quiet.

It happened in the laundry room, of all places, where she had gone to retrieve a fresh blanket for the patient in Room Eight. He had followed her, claiming he wanted to stretch his legs, but the moment they were alone, something shifted in the air. She turned toward him with a teasing remark half-formed on her lips, and he stepped forward as though guided by a force older than them both.

His hand came to her cheek.

She leaned into his touch.

His thumb brushed the corner of her mouth, and her breath caught.

And then he kissed her.

Slowly. Reverently. Like he was afraid the moment might break if he moved too quickly.

She kissed him back like she had waited lifetimes for it.

It was not passionate. Not hurried. Just two mouths discovering that they belonged. Just two people remembering each other in silence.

When they pulled apart, she didn't step back.

He didn't apologize.

She pressed her forehead to his and whispered, "I don't understand what this is."

And he said, "Maybe we're not meant to. Maybe we're just meant to feel it." She closed her eyes.

And for a moment, the war outside the walls of the hospital didn't exist.

There was only this. Him. Her. And the quiet hum of something that felt a lot like forever.

*****

The rain came on a Thursday.

It started just before dusk, a low roll of thunder grumbling along the horizon, followed by soft drops against the windows of the ward— tentative at first, like fingers testing glass. By nightfall, it was a downpour, steady and rhythmic, washing the streets in silver and turning the hospital windows into mirrors.

The woman's shift had ended hours earlier. She should have gone home. But instead, she lingered. Some excuse about reorganizing the supply closet. A chart to finish. She told herself it was coincidence that she passed him in the hallway near the back entrance just as he was slipping out of his coat.

He stopped when he saw her.

Neither of them spoke.

She held the silence between them like a question, her fingers curled around the closet's doorknob, her breath shallow.

He reached out his hand.

Not demanding.

Just offering.

And she took it.

They ran through the rain like children, laughter caught in their throats, hands clasped so tightly she could feel the bones of his knuckles. The storm soaked them through in seconds—her blouse clinging to her skin, his shirt plastered to his back. They ducked into the barn behind the empty chapel, breathless and dripping, hearts hammering against ribs that had forgotten how to protect them.

He looked at her like he had lifetimes ago in the garden.

Like she was everything.

She stepped toward him, and he caught her waist with both hands, pulling her gently, as though testing if she was real. She reached for his collar, tugging him closer, their mouths crashing together not with violence, but with vital urgency.

Rain beat against the roof overhead.

She tasted like salt and rain and everything he had ever wanted.

He kissed her as if he had no more time.

She kissed him like he was her air.

When he pushed her gently against the wall, their breath tangled, mouths parting and meeting again in dizzying rhythm. His hands trembled as they found the edge of her soaked blouse, sliding beneath it to trace the line of her back. Her fingers moved to his buttons, clumsy and desperate, pulling him free of the fabric that separated them.

She gasped as he pressed against her, their hips aligned, his breath hot against her neck.

They sank to the floor together, slow and certain, finding balance in the hollowed silence of the chapel's forgotten barn. Her knees curled around his waist. His hands cradled her face as if she might slip through his fingers. He entered her in one breathless movement, and she broke beneath him —not from pain, but from the unbearable rightness of it.

He moved gently at first, his rhythm a prayer. But her hands clutched at his shoulders, her heels dug into the backs of his legs, urging him closer, deeper. She whispered things she didn't know she'd known—fragments of promises and lifetimes and names she hadn't spoken in centuries.

And he answered every single one with his body.

The height of their passion was a moment suspended. Weightless. Infinite. After, they lay tangled in the hay, her head on his chest, the sound of the rain softening around them.

He traced lazy circles on her arm.

She listened to the steady thrum of his heart.

Neither of them said forever.

But they felt it.

And in the hush that followed, she whispered into his skin, "Don't go."

He didn't answer.

He only pulled her closer.

As if he could hold off the orders he sensed were coming.

As if he could hold back where war would take him.

As if loving her now might somehow keep him from the hell across the Atlantic in Europe.

They slept there, just for a while.

When she woke, the storm had passed. The barn was dim and quiet, filled with the scent of hay and cedar and rain. She lay still for a moment, her head rising and falling with the rhythm of his breathing, his hand still resting in her hair. For the first time in months—maybe longer—she felt warm.

Whole.

She pressed a kiss to the centre of his chest, right over his heart, and he stirred beneath her.

"We should go," he murmured, voice husky from sleep and tenderness. She nodded, but neither of them moved.

When they finally rose, they dressed slowly, eyes on each other more than the buttons and cuffs. There was something reverent in the way she smoothed his collar. Something final in the way he brushed his thumb across her cheek.

They parted in silence, slipping back into the dark, into the hospital, into their separate worlds.

The next morning, his orders arrived.

He would leave in two days.

He didn't tell her right away.

Instead, they walked the river's edge that evening, the sky above them pale and starless. The air was crisp, scented with the beginning of winter, the trees bare and black against the last of the light. She slipped her hand into his without a word, and he squeezed it so tightly she thought her bones might break.

When he finally told her, her steps faltered.

"But you just got here," she whispered.

He nodded once. "And now I have to go."

Her breath turned to frost between them. She looked at the ground, her eyes burning, her voice thick. "How long?"

"They didn't say."

Of course they hadn't.

She nodded. Once. As if she could make peace with something she would never forgive.

That night, she wrote him a letter.

She didn't know why. Maybe she hoped he'd carry it with him like he had the first one—the one he wouldn't let go of. The one he'd written to her impossibly, before they even met. The one she now kept with her. Maybe she needed him to have something to hold when she wasn't there.

She tucked it into the inside pocket of his coat while he slept, her fingers brushing the wool gently.

The morning he left was so ordinary it felt cruel.

No ceremony. No send-off.

Just the rumble of the transport truck outside the hospital, the scent of coffee in the corridors, the shuffle of nurses on shift change.

She met him in the side yard, hidden from view, their last minutes together held in the hush of bare branches and brittle wind.

He kissed her once. Deeply. Like he meant it to last.

And when he pulled back, his eyes were already wet.

"I'll come back," he said.

"You'd better," she whispered, trying to smile.

He took one step away, then paused.

"Find me again," he said softly.

She nodded, even though her heart was breaking.

"Always."

She watched him climb into the truck, watched it pull away, watched the road long after the dust had settled.

She stood there until the cold made her hands numb.

She stood there until she couldn't.

And then she turned, and walked back into the hospital.

Back into the world.

Alone.

*****

Winter came quickly after he left.

Snow dusted the rooftops by the first week of December, and the town felt even smaller beneath the grey sky. She kept to her routines—waking early, tending wounds, moving from bed to bed with practiced care. But something had been carved out of her. Something soft and glowing.

She kept his letter beneath her pillow.

And when no one was looking, she held it to her chest.

The nurses teased her gently, the way women do when they sense love without needing to name it. They didn't ask questions. She was grateful for that.

Every night before bed, she traced the memory of his hand against hers.

Every morning, she listened for the post.

Weeks passed.

And then—

A letter arrived.

But not from him.

It came folded inside an official envelope, the corner of it stamped in black. Her name was written in unfamiliar ink. She read it in the quiet stairwell outside the surgical ward, alone, the smell of antiseptic clinging to her sleeves.

It wasn't long.

They never were.

We regret to inform you...
Missing in action.
Presumed dead.

The paper shook in her hands, though her body stayed still.

She didn't cry.

Not right away.

She simply sat down, slowly, like a marionette whose strings had been quietly severed.

She read the letter again. Then again. As if somehow the words might rearrange themselves. As if somehow the ending might change.

But it never did.

He was gone.

She walked home in the snow that night without her coat buttoned, her collar turned up against the wind. The stars were bright above her, scattered like whispers across the dark.

She stood on her porch for a long time.

And when she finally stepped inside, she left the door open behind her. As if he might still come home.

As if he might still find her.

It had been the kind of afternoon that felt like a held breath.

Warm and golden. Slow with the promise of something. The city pulsed gently in the heat—buses sighing at corners, air conditioners humming behind open windows, trees tossing their early spring leaves in light too soft to sting. The sidewalks shimmered with the faint residue of a morning rain, and the breeze smelled faintly of lilac and coffee.

He walked with two takeaway cups cradled in a cardboard tray, sleeves damp with condensation. One was his usual. The other was a new roast the barista had convinced him to try. "better get my usual too," he had said. "In case you are wrong about this new blend."

The scent of espresso curled into the air. Wind chimes sang faintly from a balcony above, delicate and half-tuned. Somewhere nearby, a piano was playing—a single melody, no words, just a voice of its own rising from the open window of a brownstone stoop.

He wasn't thinking of anything in particular.

Just the weight of the cups in his hands.

The sweat at the base of his neck.

The soft ache that had lived just beneath his ribs for as long as he could remember.

And then—

He saw her.

She stood just outside the corner bookstore, her back pressed against the warm brick, one foot lifted behind her as she balanced idly on the edge of the curb. A cone of pistachio ice cream was tilted in her hand, pale green and delicate, already beginning to melt. She caught a runaway drip with the edge of her thumb and laughed to herself—quiet, off-guard, like the world had done something unexpectedly kind.

Her hair was pulled into a loose knot. Strands escaped in soft waves around her face. Her sunglasses were perched on top of her head, and she wore a sundress the colour of sunshine.

That was when it happened.

Not recognition. Not exactly.

But a shockwave of *knowing*.

It wasn't her face. It was the way the light hit her cheek. The way she stood. The curve of her laugh in the air.

He slowed. Stopped.

Everything else kept moving—the wind, the music, the low roar of a delivery truck turning down the block—but for him, the moment lengthened. Softened. Sharpened.

His breath caught. His body tensed, not from fear, but from gravity.

She turned her head, slowly, like she'd felt it too.

Their eyes met.

And in that half-second, the world paused.

The ice cream. The piano. The wind threading through the pages of books set out on sidewalk tables.

Everything held its breath.

She stared at him.

And in her eyes—something flickered.

Recognition.

Or fear.

Or the impossible echo of both.

He opened his mouth. Just to speak. Just to say—anything.

But a bus passed between them. Groaning at the gears, loud and clumsy and sudden.

When it cleared—she was gone.

Gone into the store. Or down the block. Or back into the part of the world that didn't quite believe in things like fate.

He stood there, stunned, two coffees cooling in his hands.

He crossed the street anyway.

The bell over the bookstore door didn't chime.

The shop was dim.

Empty.

Dust drifted in the still air. Somewhere in the back, someone flipped a page.

He stood in the doorway for a long time, heart hammering.

He didn't know her name.

But something in him whispered it anyway.

Please. Just once more.

Just long enough to remember.

The town unfurled beneath the summer sun like something out of a postcard, all soft corners and slow hours.

Jim Thorpe sat nestled in the crook of the mountains, its rooftops dappled in light, its streets warm with the hush of July. The trees along Broadway were lush and green, their leaves trembling in the faintest breeze, casting shadows that danced across the sidewalks. Hanging baskets of petunias swayed outside shop windows, and the scent of warm pavement, cut grass, and something sweet from the bakery on Race Street mingled in the air.

Everything here felt sun-kissed.

Even the quiet.

The train tracks at the edge of town shimmered with heat, and the bell above the diner door chimed with a slow, deliberate rhythm, announcing comings and goings that didn't seem in any particular hurry. Time moved differently in Jim Thorpe. It didn't rush. It didn't demand.

It strolled.

And for the woman, who had spent most of her life pressed into corners, the stillness of it all was like sipping on water she didn't know she'd needed. She had arrived the week before, her suitcase scuffed and her plans uncertain, a borrowed room above her cousin's hardware store and a promise to stay for just the summer.

She wasn't running away, not exactly.

She just didn't want to be found.

She spent her mornings wandering. Coffee from the corner café, sipped slowly on the bench outside the library. Afternoons lying on the grassy banks near the river, watching dragonflies skim the surface of the water, a paperback novel open in her lap. And when the sun dipped low and the streetlights blinked on, she would walk the neighbourhood just to feel the evening on her skin—bare arms kissed with humidity, the sound of someone's radio playing Elvis Presley behind a screen door.

She did not expect her heart to change.

She did not expect *him*.

And that was the beauty of it, really.

Because the most unforgettable loves are the ones we never see coming. They arrive like dusk in a quiet town—softly, slowly, and, somehow, all at once.

*****

It happened on a Tuesday.

She had taken the car out for a drive, one of those borrowed things with squeaky brakes and a loose door handle, the kind that shivered when it climbed hills. The air was thick with the kind of heat that made everything feel syrup-slow, and the sky pulsed soft blue overhead, not a single cloud in sight.

She was heading back from Mauch Chunk Lake, skin still damp from swimming, her sandals tossed onto the passenger seat beside a bottle of

Coke she hadn't finished. A fly buzzed somewhere near the dashboard, and the smell of lake water clung to her arms like perfume.

Then the engine stuttered.

Once.

Twice.

A heavy cough, and the car rolled to a halt in front of the garage on the corner of Broadway and Pine.

She sighed and leaned back against the seat, one hand brushing her damp hair from her cheek, the other resting against the steering wheel.

That was when he stepped outside.

He wore a white undershirt smudged with grease and a pair of work pants that clung to his hips in the way that made her throat go dry. His arms were golden from the sun, the kind of tan you didn't earn in a few weeks. A rag was tossed over his shoulder, and a crescent wrench dangled loosely from one hand.

He paused when he saw her.

Not dramatically. Just long enough.

As if something behind his eyes had shifted. As if the air around them had changed.

He walked toward her with slow steps, not rushed, not cocky. His boots made a steady sound against the pavement, and she watched him the whole way, unable to look anywhere else.

She rolled the window down further.

"Bit of trouble?" he asked, voice friendly and unhurried.

She shrugged, a small smile tugging at the corner of her mouth. "Seems she's given up on me."

He smiled, and the sun caught in his eyes like gold dust.

"I can take a look."

She popped the hood.

He leaned over the engine, arms flexing, eyes squinting against the light. She watched him while he worked, the strong lines of his jaw, the way his fingers moved like he was coaxing something back to life.

And for a moment, the world felt quieter.

She didn't know his name.

But she knew his hands would feel like home.

And that was the beginning.

He fixed the car, of course.

Or maybe it fixed itself just for him.

She never did ask exactly what the problem had been. After a few minutes he closed the hood with a solid thud, wiped his hands on that same rag, and told her it would start now. She'd nodded, grateful, and thanked him with a smile that felt fuller than it should have.

She hadn't expected him to walk around to the passenger side and lean on the door.

"You from around here?" he asked.

"Just for the summer."

He nodded, thoughtful. "Too bad."

She tilted her head. "Why's that?"

He hesitated, then smiled again. Slower this time.

"Because summers end."

The silence stretched between them, warm and thick.

She didn't break it.

She just looked at him.

Really looked.

And he looked back like he didn't want to blink.

That night, she drove past the garage again. Not on purpose. Or maybe exactly on purpose.

The lights were still on.

And he was there, leaning against the doorway with a bottle of soda in one hand and his eyes on the stars.

She didn't stop.

But he raised the bottle to her as she passed.

And she didn't stop smiling until she was already home.

The next day was slow with heat.

The kind of heat that softened everything—the edges of rooftops, the grip of time, the rhythm of thought. Birds sang from somewhere deep in the trees. The river moved slow and sleepy. And the woman sat on the back steps of the hardware store, a glass of lemonade dripping condensation onto her knee as she watched the afternoon pass like a dream she hadn't quite woken from.

She hadn't seen him since last night.

Not really.

But she had felt something ever since. Like a thread had been tugged loose in her chest. Like the world had tilted a fraction toward something she didn't yet have the words for.

So when the screen door creaked open and her cousin stepped outside with a raised brow and a set of car keys dangling from one hand, she didn't ask questions.

"He's asking after you," her cousin said, not unkindly.

She blinked.

"Mechanic boy," he added, smirking. "Said he thought you might like to see the view from the ridge tonight."

Her heart leapt before she could stop it.

She took the keys with a murmured thanks and slipped back inside to change.

*****

The drive was slow and winding, each turn revealing more of the valley bathed in honeyed light. The sun was beginning to set, casting long shadows across the fields, gilding the tops of trees with gold.

He was waiting by the fencepost at the end of the lane, one boot hooked over the other, arms crossed over his chest like he'd been standing that way forever. But when she pulled up, he stood straighter.

She stepped out barefoot, the hem of her sundress grazing her calves. She hadn't bothered with makeup. Just a soft curl in her hair and a spritz of something floral she barely remembered the name of.

He opened the passenger door without a word.

They drove.

No destination. No map. Just music low on the radio and the windows down. Her bare feet on the dash. His hands resting on his thighs, tanned and strong. The road ahead stretched empty and open, and the sky turned pink like it was blushing.

They didn't speak much. Just pointed things out as they passed—look at the colour of that barn, did you see the way the light caught that window?—and let the rest hang between them like lace.

When they reached the ridge, she cut the engine.

The silence was complete. Not heavy. Just full.

The air smelled like pine and dust and something faintly metallic, like the scent of distant rain.

She climbed out first, walking to the edge of the overlook, arms wrapped around herself not because she was cold, but because her heart suddenly felt too big for her body.

He came to stand beside her.

The sky unfurled before them.

She turned to say something. She wasn't sure what.

But he was already looking at her.

And she forgot whatever it was.

His hand came up slowly, fingertips brushing her jaw, featherlight.

He tucked a curl behind her ear. Let his thumb trace the curve of her cheek.

And then, slowly—achingly—he leaned in.

The kiss was like the town itself.

Slow.

Sun-warmed.

Endless.

She let her hands slide into his hair. He pulled her closer, one hand splayed against the small of her back, the other tangled in her skirt like he didn't want to let go.

The sun slipped behind the hills.

And still, they kissed.

And kissed.

And kissed.

As if they had all the time in the world.

Even if they didn't.

*****

The sun had long since vanished by the time they climbed back into the car.

The air was thick with heat and silence, the kind that made every breath feel deeper. Crickets had begun to sing low in the grass, and the sky was an inky velvet above them, scattered with stars that blinked like secrets.

She sat with one leg tucked beneath her on the passenger seat, her head resting against the backrest, her eyes half-lidded and dreamy. He looked over at her, hands still on the wheel though they hadn't moved yet.

"Wanna keep driving?" he asked, voice soft.

She nodded, and that was all it took.

They rolled down through the dark, back onto the long stretch of county road where no one passed and no one watched. The headlights caught the dust in the air like fireflies. He reached across the seat and found her hand without looking, and she laced her fingers through his like it was something she'd done a hundred times before.

They turned down a gravel path, almost hidden beneath the canopy of trees. The tires crunched slowly, carefully. At the end of the lane, tucked into the shadows, stood a lakeside cabin—old and quiet and humming with the memory of summer nights.

He parked beside it and cut the engine. The sudden stillness felt intimate.

The only sounds were the chirping of frogs and the lapping of water against the dock.

He got out first and came around to open her door. She stepped into the night, barefoot again, the stones of the path warm beneath her feet. He unlocked the cabin, holding the screen door for her, and she stepped into the darkness with a flutter in her chest.

Inside, it smelled like cedar and lake water and a little bit like dust. He lit a lamp—just one—and golden light bloomed across the wooden walls.

She turned toward him.

And the moment thickened.

They stood there, breath shallow, distance between them barely more than a whisper.

He reached for her slowly. Gently. Like she was breakable.

She met him halfway.

Their kiss, this time, was deeper.

Hungrier.

Their mouths met like a promise that had waited long enough. Her hands slid under the hem of his shirt, palms against warm skin. He groaned softly, low in his throat, and tugged her closer, their bodies flush.

Clothes peeled away piece by piece, tossed gently to the side. There was no rush, but no hesitation either. Only gravity.

Only need.

He laid her down on the old sofa, the cushions soft and worn, and kissed his way down her neck, across her collarbone, the swell of her breast. Her breath caught, and she arched beneath him, her body already aching.

His name wasn't on her lips.

But something timeless was.

She wrapped her legs around him, drawing him in, and when he entered her, the world went quiet.

The only sound was their breath, tangled and urgent.

The only light was the lamp flickering on the table.

The only truth was that in this moment, they belonged to no one but each other.

They moved slowly.

Deeply.

Every movement a question.

Every sigh an answer.

Afterward, he pulled her against him, his chest rising and falling beneath her cheek, his fingers tracing soft patterns across her back.

She closed her eyes.

And for a moment, she believed in something more than summer.

She believed in always.

Even if it couldn't last.

*****

The morning came slowly.

Light crept in through the grimy windows, golden lines, dust floating gently in the still air. The lake outside was quiet, a glassy mirror reflecting the pale blue of the sky and the soft green fringe of trees along the far bank. Somewhere, a loon called. The sound drifted through the open window like it belonged to the dream they were still half inside.

She woke first.

She lay still for a long time, her cheek against the warm skin of his chest, her fingers curled beneath her chin. The steady rhythm of his breathing was the only sound in the room besides the gentle lapping of water and the occasional creak of the cabin settling deeper into the morning.

She watched the light shift across the ceiling, pale and soft and warm, and let her mind wander in the quiet.

There was no urgency.

No ticking clock.

Just the gentle hum of being alive beside someone who felt like something she might never deserve—but couldn't imagine letting go of.

Eventually, he stirred.

Not all at once.

Just a breath drawn deeper. A hand sliding across her spine, resting low at the base, pulling her just slightly closer. She tilted her head to look at him.

He smiled.

Sleep-soft and crooked.

"Morning," he said, voice rough like gravel warmed by the sun.

"Hi," she whispered.

He reached up and brushed her hair back from her face, fingers lingering at her temple. Then he leaned forward and kissed her forehead, slow and sure.

Neither of them said anything more for a while.

There was no need.

They stayed tangled together on the couch until the sun rose high enough to fill the room. Her legs draped over his, his thumb tracing lazy circles along her hip. At some point, she dozed off again, lulled by the sound of birds and his heartbeat under her ear.

Later, they moved together in the kitchen. Barefoot and barely dressed, they cooked breakfast with the windows open wide. She stood at the old stove, flipping eggs in the skillet, while he leaned in the doorway with a mug of coffee and a look in his eyes that made her toes curl.

They ate on the porch.

Cross-legged on the steps, plates in their laps, knees brushing.

Every few minutes, one of them would glance at the other like they still couldn't believe it.

Still couldn't believe this.

And in that golden hush, wrapped in lake air and sunlight and everything that felt impossibly good, neither of them spoke of the end.

Because to speak of it would make it real.

And for now, they still had time.

They still had the morning.

They still had each other.

*****

The days that followed were quiet in the way only summer and young love can be.

They moved through the hours and the days like people caught in a dream —slow, golden, always brushing fingertips against the edge of something real. Mornings were made of lake water and bare shoulders, sunlight breaking across their skin as they swam in silence. Afternoons stretched into long drives with the windows down, her hair tangled in the wind, his arm resting over the steering wheel, music playing low and lazy between them.

At night, they lay in the grass behind the cabin, fingers laced, eyes turned to the stars. They didn't talk much about the future. They didn't need to.

There was only this.

The taste of lemon and salt on her lips after a kiss. The hum of cicadas. The warmth of his hand on her thigh. The scent of pine sap in his hair when he fell asleep with his face tucked into her neck.

Once, she told him she had never felt so free.

He smiled, like he knew. Like he had, too.

And then came the last night.

It didn't feel like goodbye. Not at first.

They'd driven into town late to grab milkshakes from the diner—two straws, one cherry. He'd kissed her behind the soda machine while the waitress pretended not to see. She had laughed when he lifted her onto the hood of the car and swore the stars were brighter just for her.

He'd said he had something to take care of. Just a quick run to the next town over. A favour for his brother. Nothing big.

He took her back to her cousin's. He promised to be back by midnight. She watched the taillights vanish down the road.

She thought about waking up with him again, back in his cabin.

She thought about the way he whispered her name.

She thought about love.

It was nearly midnight when the phone rang upstairs. The old rotary one, bolted to the hallway wall, the one her cousin never answered after ten. But it rang anyway—shrill and wrong and endless. She sat up in bed, heart already racing, the echo of it vibrating through her chest.

She reached the receiver before the fourth ring.

It was a stranger.

His voice was low. Stunned. The words slow to form.

There had been an accident.

The car.

The curve near the reservoir.

He had swerved to miss a deer, they thought. Or maybe something else. No one knew for certain. The tires had slipped in the loose gravel. The old car had rolled twice. Then fire.

And he—

She didn't remember the rest.

Just the sound the phone made when it hit the floor.

Just the silence that filled the room afterward.

Just her own breath, sharp and uneven, echoing off the walls.

She ran.

Barefoot, nightgown clinging to her legs, feet slapping the hardwood stairs. Out the door, down the street, past the diner and the closed-up garage, all the way to the place where the road curved just wrong—where the world had taken him from her.

There were still flames when she arrived.

Still smoke.

The heat curled up from the wreckage, soft and ghostly. The firemen were quiet now. One of them looked up when he saw her, but he didn't say a word. He just lowered his eyes again.

She walked forward, slowly, until the glow of the fire lit her skin.

And then she collapsed.

Right there, on the gravel.

On the road where they had once driven with the windows down and the music up, where he had told her she was the kind of beautiful that a man never forgets.

The stars spun above her.

But she didn't look up.

She only stared into the fire and whispered his name like a prayer.

And the wind carried it into the trees.

*****

The town didn't speak of it much after.

A tragic summer accident.

That's what they called it.

The kind of thing whispered in grocery store aisles and on front porches, before someone changed the subject. The kind of thing that left flowers wilted on a roadside, and a girl with salt-dried tears pressed into her skin like something permanent.

But she remembered.

She remembered the taste of his mouth, the sound of his laugh, the way his hand curled instinctively around hers in his sleep.

She remembered the heat of that last kiss and the hum of the radio and the golden dust in the air when he told her she was it. That if this was all they got, it would be enough.

And still, it hadn't been.

Every year, when the air thickened and the cicadas began to sing, she found her way back to that town, to that road.

She would walk barefoot through the grass, skirt brushing her ankles, shoulders bare to the sun, like she had that summer. She would stop at the bend where the trees pressed close and the gravel still bore the faintest black scar.

And she would sit.

And wait.

And listen.

Because something in her could not let go.

Not of the car's roar as it passed.

Not of the way he kissed her like it meant forever.

Not of the hollow ache in her chest that never healed.

Because part of her still believed—

That if she loved him hard enough, if she waited long enough, if she wished with her whole body—he might come back.

Even just for a moment.

Even just to say goodbye.

And in the silence, in the wind that stirred the trees and wrapped around her ankles like memory—

sometimes it felt like he did.

It happened on a Wednesday.

Not a dramatic day. Just grey and quiet and ordinary.

The kind of day where the wind carries the memory of something lost.

The kind of day that doesn't feel like anything—until it does.

She was browsing the shelves of a second hand bookstore tucked between a bakery and a florist, the kind of place with handwritten signs and creaky floorboards that gave beneath your steps like the shop itself had a memory of every reader who'd ever passed through. The bell over the door had chimed softly behind her when she entered, and now jazz played low from a speaker near the counter. Outside, the rain had just begun, tapping against the windows in a soft, persistent rhythm. It made the world feel smaller. Quieter.

She wasn't looking for anything.

Not a book. Not a person.

But something in her had been restless for days. Dreams she couldn't shake. Faces she couldn't name. A river in moonlight. A dance that ended in silence. A burning courtyard. A silver dagger. A peony, crushed and pink, falling from someone's hand.

A man's voice saying, *find me again.*

She shook the thought away and turned down a narrow aisle.

And there he was.

He stood at the far end of the row, one hand resting on a worn leather-bound book. His profile was turned toward her, his brow furrowed in concentration. His hair was slightly damp from the rain, curling just above his collar. He hadn't seen her yet.

But she saw him.

And her body froze.

She felt it in her knees, in the hollow of her chest, in the soft drumbeat of her heart. That impossible ache.

The same man.

From the train station.

From the flower market.

From something much, much older.

His head lifted.

And when their eyes met this time, neither of them looked away.

Her breath caught. His lips parted.

The world slowed.

She took a step forward. He mirrored it.

No crowd passed between them.

No timing broke the moment.

Only silence.

Only the quiet thud of recognition.

He opened his mouth. Then closed it.

"Do I know you?" he asked.

It was such a human question. Too small for what she felt. Too simple for what was cracking open beneath her skin.

"I think," she whispered, "you always have."

And then something fragile inside her broke open, and light poured through.

They stood there, blinking at one another like survivors.

Of what, they didn't know.

But they knew it had been *long*.

*****

They sat in the café next door, steam curling from cups of tea neither of them touched. The rain came harder now, streaking the windows, turning the street into something blurred and unreal.

They didn't speak at first. Just watched each other, like they were waiting for something to rise up between them.

It did.

He reached into his coat pocket and pulled something out.

A single peony. Pressed between wax paper. Slightly wilted.

"I don't know why I kept it," he said.

She covered her mouth with one hand.

She was crying before she could stop it.

"I was there," she said. "At the market. I dropped it."

He nodded.

"I know."

And then he pulled out something else.

A matchbook. Faded red. Ruby's Diner printed in white.

She felt the air leave her lungs.

"I loved that place," she whispered.

"You always did."
She reached into her bag. Her hands were shaking.

She pulled out a letter. Handwritten. Edges worn.

"It started in my dreams," she said. "Then I found this tucked into a book I don't remember buying."

He took the paper from her gently.

His hands shook too.

"It's your handwriting," he said.

"I think it's yours too."

And then, like thunder breaking across the sky, it began.

Memories.

Crashing through them like light. Like fire. Like *truth*.

The garden. The romance. The ending.

The docks. The falling in love. The blood.

The hospital bed. The letter. The kiss in the barn.

The lake cabin. The smoke. The siren.

The curve in the road. The firelight on stone. The saltwater goodbyes.

The silence between lives.

The ache of always finding, always losing.

She gasped and clutched the table.

He reached for her hand.

And together—they remembered.

Every word.

Every death.

Every promise.

And all of the waiting in between.

*****

They left the café in silence, the rain forgotten, their hands clasped tight.

Neither knew where they were walking until they reached the river.

It was quiet there.

Still.

The city behind them, the water before them.

She turned to him.

"We were never meant to survive it," she said. "Not until now."

He lifted his hand, and she did too.

They pressed their palms together.

The wind moved gently across the water, lifting the strands of her hair, wrapping around them like a benediction. She looked up at the sky, blinking against the weight behind her eyes.

"Do you think," she asked, "this is our last time?"

He didn't answer. He only reached for her.

The kiss was slow. Certain. A thing remembered, but entirely brand-new.

They stood wrapped in each other until the sky dimmed.

Until the city lights glimmered behind them like stars reborn.

Until the hush of the river began to sound like a heartbeat.

*****

They didn't go far.

Just across the street. Just up a staircase. Just through a door she'd never noticed before.

Inside: brick walls and warm lamplight. A narrow bed. Books stacked like monuments. A record player humming something low and sad.

He poured her a glass of wine. Set it on the windowsill.

She undressed slowly. He watched like it was holy.

And when he reached for her, it was not with hunger.

It was with awe.

He kissed her shoulders. Her throat. The curve of her spine.

He whispered her name like a vow.

She pulled him to her like prayer.

When they lay together, it was not with fire.

It was with peace.

He moved over her with reverence. She rose to meet him with grace.

There was no rush. No urgency.

Only the quiet unfolding of a promise kept and a meeting. Time after time.

Their bodies tangled, breathed, became.

When he entered her, it felt like remembering.

When they climaxed together, it felt like return.

And when they lay afterward, forehead to forehead, her palm pressed to his heart—

The cycle was already broken.

They had found each other.

And this time—

They would not let go.

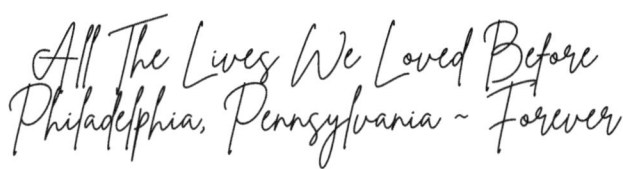

The sun broke over the city.

It poured through the high windows of 30th Street Station in ribbons of gold, illuminating dust in the air, casting long shadows across the marble floor. The same floor where she had once stood with a cup of cold coffee and the ache of almost-recognition humming beneath her skin. The same place where she had first seen him—not for the first time, but for the beginning that would finally last.

They were married there.

Not with fanfare. Not with pews or pewter goblets or organ hymns. Just the light. Just the echoes of footfalls. Just the quiet breath of a city bearing witness.

She wore white. Not a gown from a boutique, but a silk dress passed down from her grandmother—the one with sleeves that felt like falling petals. Her hair was pinned with a single peony. He wore a linen suit, soft grey, with a coin in his pocket and a small scar visible on the back of his head.

They wrote their own vows.

Not from scratch, not entirely. They had whispered them in other lifetimes. In cathedrals and cabins, in hospitals and doorways, in silence and in firelight.

"I will find you again," he said.

"And I will stay," she answered.

93

They slipped rings onto fingers that had carried other names, other fates, other endings.

This one held.

A few guests stood in a soft semi-circle, their faces blurred with tears. Someone played a cello. Someone else sang a low, wordless song that had no beginning and no end.

And when they kissed, the station exhaled.

No train arrived.

No bell rang.

Only stillness.

Only light.

Only the echo of every yes they had never gotten to say.

Later, at the reception tucked into a greenhouse café filled with climbing ivy and long wooden tables, they danced barefoot on tiled stone. Their fingers were inked with symbols now: a dagger, a rose, a constellation, a date. Tiny tattoos whispered into skin, telling stories that no one else would understand. But they would.

They always would.

He kissed the inside of her wrist.

She closed her eyes and held him closer.

There was no more searching.

No more waiting.

They had loved in every life.

And this time—

They got to live their love.

—The cycle was already broken.

They had found each other.

And this time—

They would not let go.

You've reached The End But...
The Stories Never Stop

Songs To Stories is exactly what is sounds like - short, emotionally devastating, romantically charged, and occasionally unhinged novellas inspired by the one and only Taylor Swift. Because why simply listen to a song when you can spiral into an entire fictional universe about it?

A new novella drops the 13th of every month, so if you have commitment issues, don't worry - you don't have to wait long for your next dose of heartbreak, longing, and characters making wildly questionable life voices in the name of love.

To keep up with the latest releases, visit BrittWolfe.com - or don't, and risk missing out while the rest of us are already crying over the next one. Your call.

See you at the next emotional wreckage.

About The Author
Britt Wolfe

Britt Wolfe was born in Fort McMurray, Alberta, and now lives in Calgary, where she battles snow, writes stories, and cries over Taylor Swift lyrics like the proud elder Swiftie she is. She loves being part of a fan base that's as passionate as it is melodramatic.

She's married to a smoking hot Australian (her words, but also probably everyone else's), and together they parent two fur-babies: Sophie, the most perfect husky in the universe, and Lena, a mischievous cat who keeps them on their toes—and their furniture in shreds.

When Britt's not writing or re-listening to "All Too Well (10 Minute Version)," she's indulging her love for reading, potatoes in all forms, and the colour green. She's also a huge fan of polar bears, tigers, red pandas, otters, Nile crocodiles, and—because they're underrated—donkeys.

Her life is full of love, laughter, and just enough chaos to keep things interesting.

 @the.banality.of.britt

 BrittWolfe.com

www.ingramcontent.com/pod-product-compliance
Lightning Source LLC
Chambersburg PA
CBHW082249120626
46555CB00009B/3020